CRIMES, COVENS & CURSES

Volume one in The Curious Case Mystery Series

Can you solve these ten mind-bending mysteries?

SARA FURLONG

How it works

Within this book, you will find a collection of 10 short mysteries full of clues and some red herrings. Once you have read a mystery and think you are ready to find out how it ends, go to the **Answers Section** of the book and find the title that corresponds to the mystery you just read. There, you will be able to read the rest of the story to find out exactly what happened and to see if you were correct.

CONTENTS

CURIOUS CASE #1

The Sword of Hawthorne

In Northern England, there is a Medieval village known as Beamich, and on the outskirts of the village, there is a castle that Lord Hawthorne once owned. The castle itself has been abandoned for nearly two centuries, and during that time, thousands of people have searched for, The Sword of Hawthorne, which is said to be hidden there. Why do so many people care to find a sword, you ask? Well, the hilt is encrusted with hundreds of diamonds, emeralds and rubies and the blade itself is made of solid gold. And more importantly, the sword is said to possess supernatural powers. It's even said that the Sword of Hawthorne can raise the dead.

One cold November morning, a group of five friends entered the village of Beamich in search of Lord Hawthorne's castle. Lindsey, Jamie, Arlo, Marcus and Evie were tourists from Canada that had come all the way to Northern England in search of the famed sword.

"So, this is the place," Lindsey said, handing Marcus the map. Jamie grabbed the map from Marcus to double-check where they were. "I can't believe our GPS doesn't work here. I'm not even getting a cell phone signal."

All five of them pulled out their phones to check. Nope, no signal. "All right, I think we need to ask for directions. The castle has to be around here somewhere." Lindsey said and began walking towards the nearest shop. "I mean, it's a castle. It can't be hard to miss!"

The group entered the shop to find it full of locals. The moment they walked in, everyone went silent and stared at them; it was a weird feeling. Evie spoke up first. "Hi, I'm Evie, and these are my friends. We are visiting from Canada, and we were hoping to check out Hawthorne Castle. Could you point us in the right direction?" Evie had no sooner finished asking the question when everyone in the store pointed in the same direction, out the window and towards the hill.

"Oh, ok, thanks. So the castle is in the hills?" Evie continued as all of the locals nodded their heads yes. "Is it far?" she continued. They all shook their heads no. "Can we get there on foot?" They nodded their heads yes. "Is there anything else we should know?" They shook their heads no.

The five friends stood stunned for a moment before silently leaving the shop. The second they were outside, the townsfolk returned to how they had been before they entered. It was…weird.

"Well, that was unsettling," Jamie said with a shiver. "Ya, it was like they were zombies or something. Unsettling." Lindsey added. The group looked back at the townsfolk one last time, then started down the path towards the mountains, where they would hopefully find the mysterious castle.

After walking for close to an hour, they noticed something in the distance. "Is that it? I think I see the castle."

Arlo pointed to a structure in the distance. It didn't really look like a castle, but it was still far away, and it was the only thing anywhere nearby that could possibly be the spot they were looking for.

Another fifteen minutes went by, and as the structure got closer, the group began to realize it was, in fact, the Castle of Hawthorne. They looked at each other concerned that maybe this wasn't the spot they were thinking it was but decided they had come this far and might as well continue.

With sore feet and a bit of frustration, the friends arrived at the front of the castle. It was so overgrown that they could barely see the entrance. "Is this it? Is this the right place?" Jamie asked, feeling very unsure about the whole thing.

Arlo and Evie were the first to the entrance of the castle; they started removing the vines and leaves from the entranceway. Jamie and Marcus joined them while Lindsey searched for more clues as to whether or not they were in the right spot.

"Guys! Come here!" Lindsey called to her friends, who stopped what they were doing and rushed over. "Look, this is Hawthorne Castle." Lindsey showed them a barely noticeable plaque on the castle's wall that confirmed they had found the right place.

Before attempting to enter the castle, the group decided

to walk around the outside to see what they could see.

They started to the left and made their way along the side of the massive building. They walked past overgrown gardens that were probably beautiful once upon a time and a stable that likely held amazing horses long ago.

Next, they arrived at the back of the castle. At the back of the castle, there was a large old door, and behind the castle, there was an overgrown area that looked like it had been used for jousting or something like that, a huge fountain full of dark, murky water and some more overgrown garden beds.

The friends snapped pictures of everything as they passed by; they continued on to the other side of the castle, where they saw several sheds and overgrown garden beds. There was also a tiny dilapidated house in the distance, probably where the groundskeeper once lived.

Feeling reassured, the group made their way back to the door and worked as quickly as possible to clear the entranceway. They had almost cleared the way when there was a loud crash. They all looked up to see the dark sky alive with lightning.

Just then, the skies opened, and rain began to pour down. Thankfully they were almost done clearing the way and could get in the door before the storm got any worse.

"Are you kidding me?! What are the odds of that?"

Lindsey said, ringing out her wet hair. "Well, we are in Northern England, so I feel like the odds are pretty good," Arlo replied before shaking out his wet hair like a dog.

It took a few minutes for the group to finish complaining about being soaked before they finally realized exactly where they were. Marcus was the first one to fully appreciate the magnitude of their discovery.

"Guys, we found Hawthorne castle. Like we actually found it! We are the first people to stand inside these walls in probably thousands of years!" Marcus was beside himself with excitement. The others were excited, but not the way Marcus was.

The first thing everyone did, once they were mostly dry, was take out their phones and start to take pictures and videos. If nothing else, their visit would get them some social media clout.

As they walked around capturing their surroundings, Jamie made an interesting discovery. "Guys! Over here, look at this."

Jamie was standing in a dark corner of the castle, and on the wall was an old scroll. It was really hard to read but seemed to contain some kind of riddle. The friends all joined Jamie to see what the fuss was about.

"Look, there's some kind of riddle or at least the

beginning of a riddle," Jamie said, showing the others. Arlo shone the light from his phone on the riddle, and Lindsey read it aloud.

"If my kingdom falls and is no more. My sword will be hidden beyond the door. Out of sight, away from eyes in a place that will never see the sunrise." Lindsey finished reading the riddle and looked at her friends.

"Ok, what does that mean?" Evie asked, somewhat exasperated. "It means the sword is here! We're in the right place. We just need to solve the riddle to find out." Lindsey was pumped now. They were so close to finding what they came for.

Marcus took a picture of the riddle, and the group continued to the centre of the room. "Ok, so where do we look? Where do we begin? I feel like the riddle didn't really tell us much." Jamie was raring to go but truthfully had no idea where to begin.

"Ok, so the riddle says two important things, beyond the door and no sunrise," Evie said, looking at the riddle again on Marcus' phone. "So it has to be behind some kind of door in a place with no windows? I'm guessing."

The group nodded in agreement that this seemed like as good of a place to start as any. The friends looked around the grand entrance hall and noticed four doorways, two on each side and two large entranceways, with no doors, at the back.

"Ok, how about we each look behind one of the doors to see if there are any windows? I will check down the two large hallways, but I doubt that is correct because that's technically not behind a door." Marcus said, taking charge of the group.

Everyone nodded in agreement. Jamie and Arlo headed to the left, Evie and Lindsey headed to the right, and Marcus headed toward the first hallway at the back.

It took about fifteen minutes before everyone was back, but the answer was the same for all of them—Windows down each hallway and lots of sunlight. Once again, they were back at the beginning.

"Ok, so none of those doors matched the clue. We must be missing something." Lindsey said, re-reading the riddle. "If my kingdom falls and is no more. My sword will be hidden beyond the door. Out of sight, away from eyes in a place that will never see the sunrise."

Suddenly Arlo had an idea. "Sunrise, not just sun but sunrise! The sun rises in the East, so maybe the door we are looking for is on the opposite side of the castle. Which way is east?"

Marcus opened the compass app on his phone. "East is that way." "So west is that way," he said, pointing to the entranceway. He continued pointing towards the back wall with no doors. "But there are no doors on that wall."

"We're missing something," Jamie said, walking towards the back wall. She looked down each of the two hallways on the back wall, and it hit her.

"Look! Look how narrow these halls are. There must be something between them. And look, there are no windows on the inside wall, only the outside wall. I think there's a secret passageway between them." Jamie said excitedly.

The friends checked down the hallways and agreed with Jamie; there had to be a secret passageway somewhere between those two hallways.

The five friends began searching the back wall for a clue as to where the passage may be; they were pressing bricks, grabbing anything hanging, and moving stones. Nothing was working.

They were getting frustrated, and Evie had had enough. Even though she knew it was going to hurt, she kicked the wall. But it didn't hurt. Instead, the brick moved in, and a passageway started to open.

Unfortunately, due to the age of the castle, it didn't open far enough. It took all five of them to push the door open just enough so they could slide one at a time inside.

Once inside, they all got their phones out and turned the flashlights on. It was dark. The only little bit of light was coming from the entrance to the passageway.

"So, the sword is hidden somewhere in here?" Arlo asked as he scanned the area with his phone.

"Nope, look at this." Lindsey illuminated another riddle on the wall. The rest of the group came over to investigate as Lindsey read the riddle aloud.

"You've come this far already, well done. But your journey to the sword has just begun. Passageways are not always as they seem. Perhaps there's another one in-between." Lindsey finished and looked at the rest of the group. Everyone had the same blank look on their face.

"What the heck does that mean?" Arlo said, half laughing. They all looked at each other, bewildered. Each of them hoped the other knew what to do, but it seemed like no one had any clue where to begin.

"Ok, let's think about this for a second. This hidden passage was between the two hallways. Maybe there's another hidden passageway in the centre of this one." Evie said unconvincingly.

The friends weren't sold on the idea, but since they were stumped, they decided to have a look. The five of them looked around the secret passageway for any sign of an opening. They concentrated their gaze on the centre of the passage since the riddle had specified in-between.

The group stomped on stones and moved debris around but like before, nothing was working. They were getting super frustrated when Marcus had a thought.

"Wait a second. I think we are going about this wrong. The riddle said in between. We need to look for a spot where two similar things are near each other, but there's a gap. Look at the columns on the wall. We need to look for any columns that are spaced differently than the others." Marcus pointed out the columns all along the walls; they appeared to all be about two feet apart.

Everyone agreed this seemed like the best plan, so they split up along the wall and began to search for spots that seemed out of place. It wasn't long before Arlo called out to the group.

"I think I found the spot. Look at this." Arlo was standing about halfway down the passage and had found a spot where the columns were four feet apart instead of two.

The others arrived and agreed that this must be the right spot, so they started looking for spots that could open the passageway. They pushed bricks and moved things but no luck.

"You know, it's funny. I didn't notice it earlier, but now, seeing where this passage is, I remember thinking that one of the halls seemed a lot shorter than the others when I was first inspecting them." Marcus said as he continued looking.

This comment gave everyone hope that this must be the spot they were looking for. All of them searched and searched, but exhaustion was starting to set in. Arlo and Jamie were the first to give up. They each decided to lean on one of the columns for a moment, just to give themselves a break.

It wasn't more than a second of leaning before the wall started to move. The pressure they put on the columns at the exact same time unlocked the secret passage that opened before them.

"Are you kidding me? I can't believe that worked!" Evie said, hugging Lindsey with excitement. The five friends entered the passageway that opened up much easier than the previous one had.

Once all five of them were inside, they began to walk deeper into the passage. As they were walking, Marcus tripped on something, and they turned to watch the entrance behind them slam shut.

The group was now alone in the dark. Arlo pulled his phone out and turned on the flashlight. "I'll use my phone first. We better not use them all, or we are gonna run out of batteries in all of our phones." Arlo led the way with the others close behind him, very close behind him.

"Look, there's something on that wall." Lindsey pointed

at what looked like a scroll. The group made their way over to it and discovered that, yes, it was a scroll, and it appeared to be another part of the riddle.

Arlo shone his light on the riddle and read it aloud. "You've made it this far. You are worthy and strong. I will tell you where my sword belongs. Cold dark water will bury it deep, and in this water, it will sleep."

The five looked at each other, confused once again. Arlo shone his light on the passageway ahead and illuminated two stone staircases, one going up and one going down.

"That must be it. It must be either in the attic or the basement. But which one?" Marcus said, puzzled. "The riddle talks about cold dark water, so I bet that's a leaky attic."

"No way, cold dark water is definitely in the ground; it has to be in the basement," Lindsey replied.

"Ok, how about some of us go up and some of us go down? Arlo and I will head upstairs." Marcus said, nodding to Arlo. "And you three can check out the basement." He said to Lindsey, Evie and Jamie. "Then we will meet back here to see what we found."

The five friends agreed and started to head up or down in search of the sword. Lindsey, Jamie and Evie started down the steep stairs as Jamie turned on her flashlight to light the way.

Getting down the stairs was sketchy, to say the least, with old broken stairs and no railings at all. Luckily the basement was not too far down. In fact, they had to duck to walk around the basement.

"Well, this is awkward," Evie said after hitting her head on the ceiling. Jamie and Lindsey nodded in agreement. The three of them walked around the basement for a few minutes before they found something promising.

"Look, is that water?" Lindsey asked, aiming Jamie's light toward the corner. The three friends walked over to discover that the strange blob in the corner was water.

"So, this must be it. This must be where the sword is hidden!" Evie exclaimed with excitement. The three of them moved closer, and Lindsey got down on her hands and knees, ready to reach into the water to see what was inside.

She was just about to put her hand in when she heard Jamie shout, "wait! This isn't the right spot; look at this." Jamie shone her light on a scroll on the wall just above the water.

"Yes, this water is dark and cold, but my sword it does not hold. Return to the last riddle and rethink your way, or in the dark water, my sword will stay." Jamie finished reading and looked at her friends.

"Well, I guess we picked the wrong direction.

Hopefully, the guys have had better luck." Lindsey said, dusting off her knees.

The three friends started walking back towards the stairs ducking their heads to avoid hitting the ceiling again.

Meanwhile, Arlo and Marcus were making their way through the attic, searching for the dark water and hopefully the sword.

"Watch where you step; there's lots of holes in the floor," Marcus said to Arlo as he almost put his foot in a small hole.

"Thanks. With all of these holes, any water up here is probably long gone." Arlo said, looking around the room.

"Look, what's that?" Marcus pointed to a large container in the corner under what appeared to be a hole in the ceiling.

Marcus and Arlo made their way toward the container, and they both could feel it; they'd found the right spot. When they got there, they looked inside, and it was, in fact, full of water, dark water.

Marcus was about to stick his arm in when Arlo stopped him. "Marcus, hold on a sec. Look at this." Marcus got up and walked over to where Arlo was.

Arlo had found another riddle, just like the girls had found in the basement. "Yes, this water is dark and cold, but my sword it does not hold. Return to the last riddle and rethink your way, or in the dark water, my sword will stay." Arlo read aloud.

The two guys looked at each other, defeated. They then made their way back downstairs to, they assumed, congratulate the girls on discovering the sword in the basement.

Of course, both groups were wrong, which they realized when they reentered the hall where they had started.

"No sword upstairs?" Jamie said to Marcus and Arlo. "Nope, nothing in the basement?" Arlo asked the girls, who shook their heads no.

"Well, where to now? We are out of riddles!" Lindsey said to her friends, who all shrugged. They were just about to give up when suddenly Evie had an idea.

"Wait! I've got it! I know where the sword is! Follow me!" Evie turned on the flashlight on her phone and started down the hallway between the stairs on the way toward the sword.

So where was the sword of Hawthorne hidden? You have all the clues you need to find it. Once you think you know the answer go to the ANSWER section of the book to find out what happened and if you're correct.

CURIOUS CASE #2

The Witch's Curse

It was an early October morning in 1691 when Jacob woke to prepare for his day. Jacob was a proud man, a family man, with a loving wife and two loving children. Jacob took great pride in his home and his family, but there was nothing Jacob loved more than his small shop that he had run since he was 18 years old.

As Jacob began to cook himself a hearty breakfast of bacon and eggs, he heard a tiny noise and little giggles in the distance. Knowing full well his children were standing behind him, thinking he didn't know they were there, he decided to join in on the fun.

"Good thing Julianna and Frederick aren't up yet. I want to make sure I have time to eat the small treat I brought home for myself before they awake." Jacob said, chuckling to himself.

Of course, Julianna and Fredrick, who were only 3 and 5 years old, could not resist the temptation of treats. "Father, we fooled you! We are up, and we would like a treat!" Fredrick exclaimed as he and Julianna ran over and hugged his legs.

"Oh, dear! I didn't realize you were listening to me. I guess I will have to share my treat with you." Jacob said, smiling at his two adorable children.

Just then, his wife, Maria, entered the room. "But not

until everyone has had a healthy breakfast," Maria said, ushering her two children to the dining table.

"Of course not, breakfast first. In fact, why don't I bring home an extra special treat from the store tonight, and we can have it with our supper." Jacob brought over everyone's breakfast and sat down to join them.

The little family ate happily together, enjoying their delicious breakfast. Once they had finished eating, Maria cleared the plates from the table as Jacob kissed everyone goodbye and headed off to start his day.

Jacob did not live far from his store; it was only a short walk before he arrived and was ready to start his day. It was only 8 am when Jacob arrived, and since the shop did not open until 9 am, he was enjoying some time to himself sorting out the shelves and preparing for the customers to arrive.

It couldn't have been more than ten past eight when Jacob heard a knock on the door. He ignored it and continued with his duties; his opening times were clearly posted, so whoever was there would soon realize they needed to come back during opening hours.

But that wasn't what happened. The knocking continued and got louder and louder and louder. Jacob called out to the person at the door, "We open at 9 am. Please come back then." But the knocking continued.

Finally, Jacob had had enough, and he walked over to the door to give the person a piece of his mind. He opened the door to see a young woman dressed in black.

"Excuse me, Miss, but we are closed. Please come back after 9 am, and I will be happy to serve you," Jacob said through the closed door.

"That is unacceptable. I need something now. It is for my sick calf. I cannot wait until 9 am." The woman said through the closed door.

Jacob looked around the mess of his store; it was in no state to have anyone inside, no matter what the reason was. "I'm sorry, miss, but you will need to return at 9 am. Now, if you'll excuse me, I must get back to work, or the shop won't be ready to open on time." Jacob began to walk away when the woman started to bang on the door hard. Too hard, in fact.

Jacob had had enough. He marched over to the door and told the young woman exactly what he thought of her actions. "Miss, you are being rude, and your actions are inappropriate. You are henceforth banned from entering my establishment; leave my property immediately."

The young woman did not appreciate the way Jacob spoke to her, "You will be sorry you wronged me, Jacob Thornberry." Said the young woman as she turned to walk away.

Jacob unlocked the door and quickly opened it. "Wait. Who are you? How do you know my full name?" He asked, feeling a sense of dread in his stomach.

"You will find out soon enough and regret the decisions you made upon this day." And with that, the young woman disappeared, leaving Jacob with a sick feeling in his stomach.

Jacob shook off the uneasy feeling and went back to his work, the store would be opening soon, and he was still unprepared. As Jacob sorted and cleaned, he couldn't get the thought of what had happened out of his mind. While Jacob was deep in his thoughts, he heard another knock on the door.

He turned around in frustration, ready to send them away, and then he noticed the time, 9:05 am. He was late opening his shop! Jacob quickly unlocked the door then went to do his final bits of cleaning as customers started to arrive.

It didn't take Jacob long to forget about the morning's events and get into the swing of the day. He spent the rest of the day helping shoppers, chatting with friends and neighbours and keeping his beloved shop beautiful.

Finally, 5 PM rolled around, and it was time for Jacob to close up shop and return home to his family. Jacob said goodbye to his last few customers, locked the door and began his short walk home.

That evening Jacob had an uneasy feeling, nothing terrible had happened, but he felt that something bad could happen at any moment. Maria noticed how ill at ease he was acting and sat beside him to try and comfort him.

"Jacob, what is wrong? I have noticed you are not yourself this evening. Did you have a bad day at work?" Maria asked gently. Jacob turned to Maria and forced a smile. "No, my love, nothing bad happened. It was just a rough day. Just one of those days, I suppose." Jacob kissed Maria on the cheek and then headed outside for some fresh air.

As he stood outside, he saw the young woman from this morning in the distance, "Hello? What are you doing here? Did you follow me home? Get out of here!" Jacob yelled as she quickly ran off.

Jacob went back into his house and locked the door. He had now gone from ill at ease to terrified. "Maria! Julianna! Frederick!" Jacob called out to his family, who appeared quickly in the sitting room.

"What's wrong, Jacob? What happened?" Maria said, trying not to sound too scared in front of her children. Jacob took a deep breath before replying. "Nothing. I want you all to stay close to me tonight. Perhaps we can have a campout in the sitting room."

The Children thought this was a splendid idea and were

off to get pillows. Maria looked at Jacob, concerned, but he quickly left the room so as not to begin an awkward conversation.

It wasn't long before the little family was all set up in the sitting room, ready for their campout, which, of course, the children were very excited about.

"This is such a great idea, father! Can we do this again tomorrow?" Frederick asked, cuddling into his pillow. "Maybe, son, but for now, try and get some sleep," Jacob replied, kissing him on the head.

Julianna and Frederick were asleep within moments, and Maria wasn't long behind them. Jacob thought it was odd how quickly and deeply they fell asleep but was happy that none of them asked too many questions, so he didn't question it.

Jacob remained restless for most of the night and finally fell asleep shortly before dawn. Even though he had slept for a few hours, it felt like only moments.

Jacob woke abruptly to the crow of the rooster. The morning was here, and although he was tired, he was relieved to have made it through the night, perhaps that woman was all talk, and nothing more would come from that horrible day.

Jacob got up quietly and began to prepare for the day, including making breakfast for his family. He figured the moment he started cooking the eggs and the bacon, his children would be right at his elbow as they were every morning.

Jacob turned to look at his family and noticed they were all still fast asleep. He smiled to himself and continued making breakfast. He would wake them when the time was right.

"Julianna, time to wake up. Breakfast is on the table." with breakfast finally ready, Jacob walked over and touched his daughter's cheek gently to wake her up, but she didn't move. Jacob said while caressing her head. But she didn't move.

He tried to wake Frederick next, "Frederick, time to get up. Frederick?" Jacob was unable to wake him either. Suddenly Jacob panicked. What was wrong? Why wasn't his family able to wake up?

Jacob shook Maria in an attempt to rouse her, but no luck. All three were asleep, but not just asleep, paralyzed in sleep. Jacob checked that each was still alive and was relieved that they each had a strong pulse and deep breaths.

Jacob quickly put on his clothes and ran out the door, desperate to find help. He ran straight to the local doctor and banged on the door. It wasn't long before the doctor's wife answered.

"Jacob? What's going on? Why are you here so early?" She asked while rubbing the sleep from her eyes. "I'm sorry, Mrs. Caster, but there is something wrong with my family; I need Dr. Caster to attend to them immediately," Jacob said, already leaving the door.

"But where are you going?" Mrs. Caster said, calling to Jacob, who was already on his way. "I have to find the woman responsible for their state. Please have Dr. Caster visit them immediately. I will join him back at my home shortly."

Jacob ran down the path towards his store. He decided that he should stop in to leave a note letting his customers know the store would not be opening on time that morning.

Jacob entered the store and began to write his note, 'dear valued customers, due to an unforeseen family emergency...' as Jacob was writing, a knock on the door broke his concentration. He looked up, and the young woman was standing there staring at him.

Jacob put the pen and paper down and went to the door. He opened it and saw the young woman holding her dead calf.

"This, this is all your fault. You are responsible for the death of this beautiful animal." The young woman spat at Jacob's feet and dropped the corpse of her dead calf in front of the door.

"Who are you? What do you want with me? I have done nothing to you. My store was not ready to be opened when you arrived yesterday. Rules are rules." Jacob was absolutely furious now. He picked up the calf and carried it around the back of the store, eager to remove it before any of his customers might see it there.

"It is interesting, but it appears to me that you are more concerned about keeping your shop clean than you are about the wellbeing of your beloved family. Don't you want to ask me about what has happened to them?" The young woman said slyly.

Jacob dropped the calf's body and returned. "What do you know about what happened to them? What did you do to them? Did you poison their food? Tell me what you did!" Jacob was now yelling with frustration.

"Silly man, I never laid a hand on them. I did not have to. My words and thoughts are powerful enough." The young woman replied calmly.

"What are you saying? Are you saying you're a witch?" Jacob asked, his blood starting to boil. "I am indeed, sir, and your family is under a curse all thanks to you and your callous behaviour." The young woman began to walk away from Jacob, but he was not about to let her go.

"Whatever you did to them, undo it now! Your issues

are with me. They did nothing to you." Jacob said, grabbing the young woman's arm.

The young woman pulled her arm from Jacob's grasp. "Yes, it is true. They are paying for your mistake, but that is the price you pay for having a family. You see, I am unable to break the spell. Only you can do that now." The young woman said, beginning to walk away.

"What? What do I have to do?" Jacob called to her, feeling more and more desperate. "It is easy. All you have to do is destroy the thing you love most. Once that is done, your curse will be lifted." And with that, the young woman disappeared into the woods, leaving Jacob alone with his thoughts.

Jacob went back into his store, locked the door and wept. What had he done? What did he need to do? Did he need to murder one of his family members to save the others? What kind of impossible decision had he been left with?

After a moment of sobbing, Jacob composed himself and finished writing the note to his customers. He put the note on the door and was about to leave when he had a thought. He went back inside, grabbed a sharp knife from behind the counter, locked up, and continued home.

Jacob entered his home to find his family exactly where he had left them and a very confused Dr. Caster standing beside them. "Jacob, I'm glad you've returned. I don't know what to tell you, but there is something deeply wrong with your family. They appear to be fine, their hearts and lungs are strong, but there is no waking them. I have tried several methods to no avail." Dr. Caster was deeply disturbed by all that was happening and could not provide comfort or hope to Jacob.

Jacob nodded his head in thanks and led the doctor to the door. He closed and locked the door, then returned to his family's side, unsure what to do next.

Jacob spent the rest of the day sitting with his family, hugging them, holding them, and speaking to them. He loved them all so dearly that he could not choose whom to sacrifice to save the others. And what if he made the wrong choice? And on top of that, he had only alerted shoppers that the shop would open late and here it was 4 PM, and the shop had not opened for one moment today.

Jacob walked around his family, looking at each of them, then suddenly, it hit him. He knew exactly what to do to save his family and break the curse.

So what did Jacob do to break the curse? You have all the information you need to figure out the answer. Once you know the answer, go to the ANSWER section of the book to find out what happened and if you're correct.

CURIOUS CASE #3

The Pirate's Revenge

For thousands of years, pirates have called the Caribbean home. Pillaging, plundering, wreaking havoc everywhere they go, it should be no surprise that even in death, pirates seek revenge.

The year was 1798, and the Caribbean was full of small islands that pirates called home, or at least a spot to hide their treasure. One of the most famous pirate islands was called Turtle Cove, and it offered absolutely everything a pirate could need. Easy water access, great hiding spots for treasure and plenty of protection from enemies.

Because this island was so popular, it was always a hotbed for fights, some of which were incredibly violent. Turtle Cove was a favourite of one pirate in particular, Captain Bartholomew Walker, better known as Bart, the Beast.

Bart the Beast and his crew arrived on the island one July morning to discover it was currently abandoned. This, of course, was a shock to the crew who had come ashore ready to fight.

"Well, me, lads. It appears we are alone, and Turtle Cove is ours!" Bart the Beast cheered loudly, and his crew replied with a hearty 'AYE!'

Bart the Beast and his crew moved fast, setting up shelters and establishing a perimeter around the island. If they were to claim it as their own, they needed to ensure that message was received by every pirate in the area.

Once the island was secure and shelters had been erected, Bart, the Beast, brought his family off the ship and showed them to their new living quarters.

Bart's wife Annabella and sons Claudio and Artemis were overjoyed to be off the ship and on dry land for the first time in many months. "Father, is this our home? Are we going to live here?" Claudio, Bart's youngest, asked.

"Yes, son. You are home, and this island will be forever ours. In fact, any pirate who dares call themselves Captain on this island will be cursed for all eternity." Bart said, ruffling Claudio's hair. Claudio and Artemis hugged their father and then ran off to play. Annabella kissed Bart on his cheek and then went off after the young boys.

Over the coming weeks, Bart the Beast worked his crew hard setting up the island and turning it into their new home. Unfortunately, as time dragged on, it became obvious that Bart the Beast wasn't just setting up a new island home. He was creating a new island kingdom.

Bart the Beast had previously only been considered a beast by those who dared cross him, but he was slowly becoming a beast in the eyes of his crew. His demands were getting more unreasonable, and his temper was growing shorter and shorter. In fact, the only people the Captain was civil to nowadays were his wife and sons.

One night, after Bart and his family had retired to their home for the evening, the crew members devised a plan. They talked, and they planned, and they plotted to overthrow Bart, the Beast, take over the island and name the first mate the new Captain.

The following day as Bart and his family rose, they were met with anger and force from the crew, determined to kill Bart, the Beast and take control of the island.

As the crew captured Bart, Annabelle and the boys managed to escape. They fled their home and everything they had in order to seek refuge on the opposite side of the island, away from the murderous pirates.

"Yar! What ya be doing to me? How dare ya mutiny against me!" Bart the Beast said as he was dragged from his home and to the island's shore.

"Bart the Beast. You have abused your power for too long. Anything to say before we run ya through?" The first mate, Carlos Peters, said with his sword held high.

"Aye. Anyone who dares call themselves Captain on this island, my island, will suffer a terrible fate. A painful death. And this will be the case for all eternity." Bart, the Beast, had barely finished speaking when Carlos Peters ran him through with his sword.

"Enough outta ya! So long, Bart, the Beast!' Carlos let Bart's body fall to the ground as all the crew members cheered. Carlos then pulled his sword out of Bart and held it high above his head.

That night, the crew held a party to celebrate the change in regime. Bart the Beast was no more; Carlos the Conqueror was their new captain!

As the group ate and drank and partied, an ill wind blew across the island. Nothing had changed that anyone could put their finger on, but something felt off.

You see, pirates are very superstitious, and even though logic told them that Bart the Beast couldn't possibly come back from the dead to exact revenge, he did promise a curse would befall the new captain.

The pirates began to drink more and more, trying to numb their minds to the thought of the curse. They partied into the early morning until every last pirate passed out.

The next morning the pirates awoke slowly. The warm sun on their faces roused them from their slumber as they prepared to start a new day, the first day with Carlos the Conqueror as their captain.

As the pirates got up and began their day, they realized they had not seen the new captain yet. Figuring he was still asleep after his long night of partying, they made their way to his home to wake him up.

They entered the home and searched for the captain, but he was nowhere to be seen. They headed back down towards the beach when they saw something in the distance that looked like a body.

The crew quickly made their way toward the body, and that's when they discovered Carlos the Conqueror dead. They rolled him over and looked at his face. It was clear he had been poisoned.

The pirates had seen enough, they didn't know how it was possible, but the curse was real. They gathered their personal belongings, boarded their ship and were gone before nightfall, never to return to the island again.

Of course, word of the curse travelled far and wide, and for years no pirates dared to set foot on Turtle Cove for fear of their captain dying from the curse.

Finally, after fifty years, a band of pirates ended up on Turtle Cove after rough seas forced them to go ashore or perish. They, of course, knew of the dangers the island held for captains, so the crew worked together to create a shelter around the captain, protecting him from danger.

The following day the crew awoke to find the captain gone. They searched the island and discovered his body on the shore, poisoned, just like the Captain 50 years ago.

The pirates grabbed their belongings and left the island, and no one has returned to the island since.

How could Bart the Beast carry out his curse even after his death? Once you know the answer, go to the ANSWER section of the book to find out what happened and if you were correct.

CURIOUS CASE #4

The Lost Pyramid

The year was 1928, and Cairo was a hotbed for adventurers, archaeologists and treasure seekers. One such man, Gerald Marrow, fell into all of these categories. He was a great adventurer who had travelled to the ends of the earth and back, a skilled archaeologist who had overseen digs across Africa and, above all else, a treasure seeker who was always looking for the next big find.

When Mr. Marrow arrived in Cairo, he had nothing but his backpack, a map and the determination to find the ancient treasure of Ra that had captured the interest of so many treasure hunters. The first thing Mr. Marrow did was check into one of the most beautiful hotels in Cairo with a magnificent view of the Nile river.

"Good afternoon, fine sir. My name is Gerald Marrow, and I would like to book a room for the week, preferably one facing the Nile." Mr. Marrow laid down a crisp American dollar with a smile.

The front desk host slipped the bill into his pocket. "Very good sir, here is your key. Room 402, a corner suite on the top floor with a beautiful view of the Nile." The front desk host handed Mr. Marrow his key, and he was on his way.

When Mr. Marrow entered the room, he was overcome by its opulence. Definitely the most beautiful hotel room he had occupied in many years. He put his backpack and map down and walked to the window to enjoy the view. The front desk host was right. This room had an exceptional view of the Nile River, exactly what he needed to begin his search.

After enjoying the view for a few moments, Mr. Marrow called down to the front desk to order a cup of tea and some cookies. While waiting for his tea, he began to pull books out of his backpack and place them on the table. "The Ancient World as we Know it, Mysteries of the Pharaohs, Unearthing the Past, Star Charts and Constellations 1925 edition." Mr. Marrow read the titles of the books as he meticulously laid them on the table.

He was just about to get his map when there was a knock at the door. Mr. Marrow made his way to the door, "Hello. Oh, that looks delicious, thank you." Mr. Marrow tipped the boy and returned to the table with his tea and cookies.

Mr. Marrow poured himself a cup of tea and enjoyed several cookies before moving his dishes to the side and unrolling his map across the table. Using his books, Mr. Marrow carefully flattened the map and looked at the details.

"And there it is, the treasure of Ra. I can't believe I am this close to being the first person to lay my eyes on it in centuries." Mr. Marrow squealed with glee, letting down his normally proper persona.

Mr. Marrow continued talking to himself. "According to

this map, the treasure of Ra is buried deep beneath the sand directly under The Ferryboat constellation." Mr. Marrow opened his Star Charts and Constellations book to the chapter about constellations over Egypt. He then flipped the pages until he reached the Ferryboat constellation.

Mr. Marrow looked up the coordinates for the constellation and then used that to guide the coordinates on the map. It wasn't long before he had completed his map and had the direction of where he needed to go, and it was not far from where his hotel was located.

Mr. Marrow practically squealed with delight as he packed up his backpack with the original map and the revised map. He then got ready for bed. Even though it was early, he knew he wouldn't have enough time to complete his journey today, so instead he figured he would get an early night and be out at first light the next morning.

It didn't take long for Mr. Marrow to fall asleep. His dreams were full of gold, treasure and fame. He was almost sorry to awaken to the reality that none of it had happened yet.

Even though it was early, Mr. Marrow was out of bed in no time. He went down to the lobby for a quick breakfast, and as soon the sun began to rise, he was hailing a car and on his way to the home of the treasure of Ra.

The car drove Mr. Marrow to the edge of the desert, where he met his guide and assistants. The four men climbed up on camelback and made their way deep into the desert beyond the great pyramids.

It was early afternoon when Mr. Marrow arrived at the spot where he expected the treasure to be hidden. Along with the help of his guide and assistants, Mr. Marrow began to dig.

It wasn't long before their shovels hit something. "The treasure!" Mr. Marrow exclaimed, throwing his shovel to the ground. Instantly he was down on his hands and knees, ready to reveal the treasure he longed to behold.

Mr. Marrow dusted away the sand, expecting to reveal a triumphant treasure but instead, he revealed a stone wall that must have been part of a structure that existed thousands of years ago.

Frustrated but unwilling to give up, the men split up slightly and continued to dig. They found nothing more than pieces of the wall they had already revealed.

The sun was beginning to set when the guide called off the expedition. They would try again tomorrow.

And they did; they tried again the next day and the next day, and the day after that with no luck. In fact, Mr. Marrow took up residence in Egypt and continued to search for the treasure for 44 years. He discovered ancient buildings, tombs and relics that are studied worldwide but as hard as he tried, he never was about to locate the treasure of Ra.

It was shortly before his 80th birthday in 1972 when Mr. Marrow decided he could no longer attempt to find the treasure himself, so he summoned his niece, Eliza, his only living relative, ready to pass on the promise of riches to her.

It was about a week later when Eliza arrived. "Uncle Gerald!" Eliza exclaimed, running over to hug her uncle. "It has been years since I last saw you! How are you? What have you been up to? You must tell me everything.!" Eliza and Gerald hugged once more before the two sat down to enjoy tea and cookies in the warm Egyptian sun.

"My dear Eliza, I'm so glad you were able to join me; I have so very much to tell you." Gerald squeezed Eliza's hand tight and then began to tell her in detail everything he had done over the last 40 years.

Eliza was flabbergasted by everything her uncle had done. "My goodness Uncle Gerald, you have had quite the adventures. I can't believe all of the things you discovered on your journeys!" Eliza noticed her uncle didn't look nearly as excited about his accomplishments as she was.

"Yes, I have seen and done so very much but the one thing I have never found is the treasure of Ra. And that is where you come in." Gerald smiled at Eliza, who was quite puzzled but smiled back.

"What did you have in mind?" Eliza asked, a little unsure of what her uncle might say. Gerald winked at Eliza and pulled out his map, books and everything he had learned about the treasure of Ra over the last 44 years.

Eliza and Gerald spent days going through the documents and maps. Gerald explained how he had calculated the location from every point on the constellation but was never able to get it to line up with the treasure.

Gerald's health had begun to fail almost immediately after Eliza arrived, and she could tell it was taking him every ounce of his strength to ensure she had all of his knowledge before he passed.

On the final morning before Gerald passed away, Eliza was up early and out the door; she had awoken with a clear vision of how to find the treasure.

Eliza hired a guide and was off into the desert shortly after the sun had risen. Eliza and her guide rode into the desert to the exact spot she had plotted on the map, and within two hours, they hit something.

Eliza and her guide dusted off the object and discovered it was a large golden box. Together, they lifted it out of the ground and, using a crowbar, pried it open.

Eliza and her guide looked at each other, and to their

shock and amazement, they had finally discovered the treasure of Ra.

They swiftly rode back to Gerald's home and raced to show him the treasure before he passed. "Uncle Gerald, Uncle Gerald, we found it! We found the treasure of Ra!" Eliza said, running to her uncle.

Uncle Gerald barely had any strength left, but the idea of the treasure was enough to rouse him. "You did it! You did it, Eliza! How did you figure out where the treasure was hidden after all these years?"

Eliza smiled and explained to Gerald exactly how she did it. Gerald laughed to himself. How could he have possibly missed something so obvious? "Thank you, sweet girl," Gerald said, clasping Eliza's hand one more time before passing away, happy.

How did Eliza find the treasure of Ra? Once you think you know the answer, head to the ANSWER section of the book to see if you were correct.

CURIOUS CASE #5

The Invasion

It was a warm summer day in 1939 when Dr. Clarke and Dr. Write were in their lab working on their latest experiment. It was late in the day, and the sun had set when something strange caught Dr. Clarke's eyes.

"Did you see that?" Dr. Clarke said, putting down the test tube he had been holding. "Hmm? What? I didn't see anything." Dr. Write replied as he continued to look through his microscope.

"Out there. There was a strange light. I think something is outside." Dr. Clarke walked over to the window to investigate further. He had a sixth sense about strange occurrences, and whatever lit up the night sky was certainly odd.

Dr. Write wasn't buying it. "It was probably just someone driving by with their lights on, but if you're worried about it, take a look." Dr. Write didn't even look up from his microscope.

"Well, maybe I will!" Dr. Clarke said angrily; he was sick of Dr. Write always being so dismissive. Dr. Clarke noisily walked out of the lab, making sure Dr. Write could feel how annoyed he was. Dr. Write didn't even flinch; being dramatic was Dr. Clarke's specialty.

Once outside, Dr. Clarke turned on his flashlight and began to inspect the area. Everything appeared to be normal.

Maybe Dr. Write was right after all. Dr. Clarke was just about to give up and go back inside when he saw something, something, unlike anything he'd seen before.

With his flashlight in hand, Dr. Clarke walked over to investigate what he was looking at because he genuinely couldn't believe what he was seeing.

As Dr. Clarke crept closer, he noticed a number of lights coming from what appeared to be a large metal tube. The closer he got, the more confused he became. Whatever this thing was, it was unlike anything he'd ever seen before.

When Dr. Clarke was a few steps away when he heard a sound and stopped dead in his tracks, he stood silently for a moment and was just about to turn around and go back when he heard a voice, "What the heck is that thing!" Dr. Write appeared out of seemingly thin air.

"Shhhhh." Dr. Clarke said, putting his hand over Dr. Write's mouth, but it was too late. No sooner had Dr. Write opened his big mouth when the large metal cylinder came to life. Four little beings, not of this world, opened the hatch and walked out of the cylinder to stand right in front of the doctors.

"What? What are those things!" Dr. Write said, hiding behind Dr. Clarke. "How am I supposed to know?" Dr. Clarke said with frustration. First, Dr. Write didn't even believe him, and now he was making the situation infinitely worse.

Dr. Clarke decided he should try and smooth things out with these beings. "Hello. I am Dr. Clarke, and this is Dr. Write. Whom might you be?" Dr. Clarke spoke clearly and calmly despite feeling anything but calm.

The four beings looked at each other and then back at the doctors. "Hello. We are Zee, Zon, Zola and Zelda from the planet you call Neptune." Said Zee in perfect English.

"Nice to meet you. May I ask how you know English if you are not of this world?" Dr. Clarke asked calmly.

"We do not know English, as you call it. We are speaking Neptunian. Our helmets are equipped with a universal translator, so you can understand us, and we can understand you." Zon explained enthusiastically.

"Wowza! You are from Neptune, the planet Neptune? And you just crash-landed here on Earth?" Dr. Write said, regaining his boisterous attitude.

"Yes, we were on our way to your planet in search of an element we require when your atmosphere proved hazardous for our spaceship," Zee said slowly.

"What exactly do you require?" Dr. Clarke asked, trying to remain calm.

The Neptunians looked at each other then Zon answered, "Plutonium, we require plutonium."

The doctors looked at each other confused. "Plu-to-ni-um?" Dr. Write said, confused.

The Neptunians looked at each other and then back at the doctors. "Yes, Plutonium. Do you not know of it? We were assured that Earth was the planet to get Plutonium." Zon was beginning to panic.

"Perhaps you meant to travel to Pluto? I would think Pluto would be the logical home of something called Plutonium." Dr. Write said, hoping to appease these odd little creatures from Neptune.

"No, you are mistaken. Earth is where Plutonium is found. Please take us to someone who would know where we could find Plutonium." Zee was getting very agitated now.

The doctors looked at each other confused. "If such an element existed, we would be the ones to know of it. But there is no such thing known as Plutonium." Dr. Clarke said, concerned for how the Neptunians might react.

"Unacceptable! Unacceptable! Are you telling us we are now trapped on this infernal planet? Unacceptable!" Zon began stomping his feet as the others moaned in anguish.

Dr. Clarke and Dr. Write slowly backed away from the crash site, then ran back to their lab and locked the door.

"My goodness? What just happened? I can't...I don't... What is going on!" Dr. Write said, starting to panic.

"I don't know! I don't know! Are we stuck with those strange creatures here forever? How are we going to get them back home? And what is this Plutonium they speak of? I don't understand any of this!" Dr. Clarke said, joining in on the panic.

So, Detective, what do you think? Plutonium does, in fact, exist, so why didn't these two brilliant scientists have any idea what the Neptunians were talking about? Once you think you know the answer, head to the ANSWER section of the book to see if you are correct.

CURIOUS CASE #6

The Forbidden Temple

The year was 1968 when a group of explorers set out to find the Forbidden Temple, deep in the heart of the Peruvian Amazon, an unforgiving jungle region in northeastern Peru.

After weeks of drudging through the dark forest, the four explorers finally came upon the temple they had been searching for.

"That's it! I think we found it!" said Peter Marks, the most senior explorer on the expedition. "From everything I have seen in my research, I believe this to be the Forbidden Temple." Peter continued pulling a book out of his backpack.

Peter flipped through the pages until he came across a sketch of the temple that looked like the one standing before them. He put the book down on a rock so the others could see.

Jack, Arwen and Sebastian all leaned in to look at the image. "You're right. That does look like this temple." Sebastian said, looking between the book and the temple.

"I'll admit it does look very similar, but no one has set foot inside the Forbidden Temple in almost 3000 years; it seems odd that an almost exact sketch of it is inside your book." Arwen, always the skeptic, wasn't totally buying it. As much as she wanted to have found the Forbidden Temple, it seemed like a pretty big coincidence.

"Well, there's only one way to know for sure; we need

to get inside," Jack said, closing the book and handing it back to Peter. The four didn't agree on much, but they did agree on that. The only way to know if they had, in fact, found the forbidden temple was to attempt to enter it.

"Why do you think no one has attempted to enter this temple in 3000 years? I mean, if the sketch is to be believed, others have been here quite recently, at least in the past hundred years or so." Arwen said as they got closer to the entrance.

"Probably because of the curse," Peter said nonchalantly as he headed towards the door. The other three stopped in their tracks. Peter realized they had stopped and turned around to face them.

"Curse? What curse? I wasn't aware of any curse." Jack said as Arwen and Sebastian agreed with him. "Your research didn't speak of any curses." He continued getting agitated.

"And why would it? My research only contained legitimate facts, and curses do not exist. I only mentioned it in passing as an explanation as to why no one else has entered the temple; they probably believed in the ridiculous notion of a curse." Peter said, continuing towards the door.

"Well? Are you going to tell us at least what the rumoured curse is? If it has kept people out of the temple for 3000 years, it must be a pretty convincing story." Arwen caught up to Peter and put a hand on his shoulder, forcing him to turn around.

"Fine, I will tell you what the rumoured curse is, but then we are going inside, agreed?" Peter said while rummaging through his backpack. The others looked at each other and nodded in reluctant agreement.

"Ok, here it is." Peter pulled a folded piece of paper out of the jacket of a book. "The Curse of the Forbidden Temple. Upon completion of the temple, the high priest's only son was murdered in the main entranceway. As he lay dying on the ground, the high priest cried in pain and swore that anyone who entered the temple would befall a terrible fate. He then buried his son within the temple and sealed the door forever, turning the temple into his son's tomb." Peter refolded the paper and placed it back in the book jacket.

The others looked at each other and then back at Peter. "Well, that's a disturbing story. Are there any more details about the curse?" Sebastian asked.

"None, that's all I could find. Now I'm sure you see why I don't believe it. It sounds more like a warning than a curse. Just a grieving father lashing out in anger, nothing more." Peter walked past the others and right to the main door.

The others had to agree; the curse didn't really sound

like much of a curse. They joined Peter at the entrance, ready to make their way inside the Forbidden Temple.

As you can imagine, opening a temple that has been sealed for 3000 years was anything but easy. It took the four explorers hours, but eventually, they managed to break the seal.

"Did you hear that? It's open!" Peter said excitedly as the four of them heaved the door open just wide enough so they could slip inside.

The smell inside the temple was almost unbearable, and there was absolutely no light at all. The four explorers turned on their flashlights and revealed the vast temple before them.

"Wow, this place is incredible. I can't believe it has been locked tight for 3000 years." Arwen said, using her flashlight to illuminate the room.

There were jewels and gold and statues and magnificent sculptures all around the main room. At first, the group was so amazed by the beauty that they almost missed the tomb of the high priest's son. That is until Sebastian fell right on top of it.

"Sebastian, are you ok?" Jack said, helping Sebastian up. "I think so," he replied, rubbing his back. "I was looking up instead of down, rooky explorer mistake," Jack continued shining a light on the tomb he just tripped over.

Arwen and Peter made their way over to join the others. "So if this is the priest's son's tomb, then the curse is real?" Arwen said nervously.

"There's some writing on it. I think I can translate." Peter said, shining his flashlight on the inscription on the tomb.

Arwen and Jack put their flashlights on the tomb so that Peter could free his hands to begin his translation. It took several minutes, but Peter was able to translate enough of the inscription to give them a clear picture of what was going on.

Peter read his translation aloud, "Here lies my beloved son. As he died, so too shall you. There is no way out. This temple will be your tomb."

The four explorers looked at each other. "Well, I've heard enough. I'm outta here." Sebastian said, heading towards the door. He was almost there when there was a loud rumble, and an indoor avalanche occurred, depositing hundreds of rocks in front of the door; they were trapped.

"We're trapped! Now what?!" Jack exclaimed in fear. Everyone looked at Peter; it was clear whom they were blaming.

"There has to be another way out. I suggest we split up and search the temple. There look to be four passageways; we can each take one." Peter said very matter-of-factly. He knew this was all his fault, but he certainly wasn't going to admit it.

The other explorers reluctantly agreed and began down the various hallways to see what each had in store.

Arwen went down the first hallway. It was small and stuffy, and completely miserable. She walked for a few minutes, and then she walked right into a wall. She felt around on the wall for any openings but had no luck; she had come to a dead end. Frustrated, she turned around and made her way back to the entrance chamber.

Jack made his way down the next hallway, which was very dark and dank. As he walked down the hall, he started to get a weird feeling in his stomach, almost as if he was falling. Luckily his instincts kicked in, and he stopped right before he was about to step into...nothing. Jack looked down and realized he was standing on the edge of what appeared to be a bottomless pit.

Jack picked up a large rock, the largest he could carry and shoved it over the edge. He waited, and waited and waited, but there was no sound, "bottomless?" he said to himself, confused. He quickly returned to the main chamber to inform the others.

Sebastian went down the third hallway and ended up at a pit just like Jack, but this pit wasn't bottomless, in fact, it was full of spikes. He reached forward to touch one of the spikes, and it was incredibly sharp, sharp enough to make his finger bleed.

Sebastian yelped in pain, echoing down the hallway and back to the main chamber. Embarrassed but otherwise fine, Sebastian put his finger in his mouth and returned to tell the others what he found.

Peter went down the fourth and final hallway. It certainly was the smelliest of the hallways, but he plugged his nose and continued. Finally, he got to the end and came across a vast pit of poisonous snakes. He examined it for a moment, then returned to the main hall to tell the others what he had discovered.

So, Detective, which hallway did they choose? The dead end, the bottomless pit, the pit of spikes or the pit of poisonous snakes? Once you think you know the answer, head to the ANSWER section of the book to see if you're correct.

CURIOUS CASE #7

The Ghost in the Attic

It was a rainy July afternoon in the summer of 1995 when three friends, Ashley, Monica and Jillian, were home alone watching television. When their show ended, they looked at each other, bored.

"What do you guys want to do? I'm so bored!" Ashley said, flopping over the back of the couch. "There's nothing to do." She continued dramatically.

"We could play a game," Monica suggested reaching for the game of Clue that was sitting next to the couch. Neither Ashley nor Jillian looked impressed. Monica set the game back down. "Well, Jillian, it's your house. What do you suggest?"

Before Jillian could answer, there was a loud noise coming from upstairs. The three friends looked at each other. "Is anyone else home?" Ashley asked nervously. "No, just us," Jillian replied, feeling more than a little scared.

The friends decided to head upstairs to see what was causing the sound. None of them wanted to be the first, so they all walked together, which wasn't easy.

When they reached the top of the stairs, they heard the noise again. "It sounds like it's coming from my parent's room," said Jillian leading the way down the hall. Monica and Ashley followed behind, close on Jillian's heels.

Jillian slowly opened the door, and the three friends

entered the room. They stood silently for a few moments waiting for the sound to happen again. Silence. Monica was just about to suggest they leave when they heard the sound again.

This time the sound seemed to be coming from above them, in the attic. "The sound is coming from above us," Monica said, looking up. "It must be in the attic," Jillian said with a shaky voice. "We've come this far; we can't stop now," Ashley said bravely.

The friends looked at each other with determination. Jillian went into the hall closet and grabbed a step stool, and brought it into her parents' closet, then climbed to the top and pulled down the ladder to the attic.

One by one, the friends made their way into the dark attic. "Does anyone have a flashlight?" Ashley asked shakily. She had barely finished speaking when a light shone so brightly it nearly knocked them all over.

"What was that?" Monica asked, shocked. "I thought you needed a light." A strange voice replied. "Who said that?" Jillian said in a panic. "It was I, did you not come up here to see me?" the voice said again.

By now, the girls were thoroughly freaked out, but Ashley somehow managed the ability to say something. "Show yourself! Who are you?" Silence. The friends looked at each other and were about to head back downstairs and get the heck out of the house when a bright light blinded them.

"I am Marisa. I committed a terrible crime in this attic 30 years ago. Please help me put things right so my soul can rest in peace." The ghostly light spoke in a shaky voice. "Pierce her heart with the sharpest blade.

A true love's soul must be saved

By flowers lay her body now

Let the truth be heard somehow."

The ghost finished speaking and disappeared. The friends were left standing in the attic, and all of the disturbances seemed to stop.

"Well, that was weird. Let's get out of here." Monica said, making her way towards the stairs, but before she could get there, the door slammed closed, trapping them inside the attic.

"We're trapped!" Monica screamed. All three girls tried with all their might to open the door but had no luck. They really were trapped. Ashley was the first to give up. She slumped down to the ground and started sobbing.

Monica and Jillian went over to comfort her. It wasn't long before she pulled herself together. "Sorry, sorry. I know crying won't help. Maybe if we figure out what happened, we'll be able to get out of here." Ashley said, wiping away her tears.

The three friends got up with a new resolve; they had to solve the mystery and get out of the attic. "Ok, let's look around to see if we can find any clues as to what happened. I'll go this way." Jillian said, pointing to the left. "I'll go that way," Monica said, pointing to the right. "And I'll search over there," Ashley said, pointing straight ahead.

The girls found a box with flashlights and then began to search the attic for clues. Over on the left side of the attic, Jillian found a huge chest. She opened it slowly and discovered tons of clothes and jewelry. She went through the clothes, and then she found something truly disturbing—a beautiful shirt with a red blood stain on it, big enough to have been deadly.

Jillian took the shirt out of the chest and laid it on the ground. She searched for another few minutes and found a knife, some women's gloves that appeared to have blood on them, some bloody handkerchiefs with the initials J.J. and three white candles that had previously been lit. Jillian closed the chest and made her way back to the entrance to show the others what she had found.

While Jillian was going through the chest, Monica was going through a box on the other side of the room. Monica found a pile of letters that were addressed to Marisa Monroe, the ghost that was holding them hostage, and a pile of letters addressed to someone named Claire Archibald.

Monica began flipping through the letters to Marisa,

and most seemed to be written by a man named Jack Jovin. The letters were dated for several years and then abruptly stopped. Monica then found Marisa and Jack's wedding photos. *I guess the letters stopped when they got married; she* thought to herself as she continued flipping through the notes.

There were a few letters from friends and well-wishers, then the letters changed to be from someone named R.D. Jillian flipped through and found dozens of letters from R.D. she opened one and read what it said inside.

"My dearest Marisa, I can't believe what they have done. We must put an end to all of this. I will leave it to you to do what you must. Good luck. R.D." Monica read the letter and noticed it was the last one, whatever happened after this letter R. D. never wrote to Marisa again.

Monica then went to the pile of letters addressed to Claire and began flipping through them. There were letters to Claire from many different people, including Michael B. Scholl, David Marsh, Oliver Thompson, Roland Matthew Derby, J.J. and Clark Davers. All of the envelopes addressed to Claire seemed to have a dried rose inside.

Like with Marisa, the letters to Claire seemed to stop abruptly. The last letter written to Claire seemed to be from Marisa. Monica went to open the envelope and noticed that the letter inside was torn up and only a tiny portion of it remained.

She tried to make out what the letter said, but there wasn't enough to really make out what it said. 'How dare you? Never forgiven, my love and die, seemed to be the only phrases Monica could make out."

Monica picked up the letters and took them back to the entrance to see what her friends thought of the unusual clue she had found.

Meanwhile, Ashley was at the front of the attic, where she discovered a most disturbing clue. "Jillian! Monica! Come here, quick!" Ashley said in a panic. Both Jillian and Monica rushed over to see what Ashley had found, bringing their clues with them.

"Look!" Ashley said, pointing at what was lying on the ground. Monica and Jillian looked down to see a skeleton. "Is that the ghost? Is that the lady that is haunting us?" Jillian asked, starting to freak out.

"I don't know," Ashley replied in a shaky voice. "It looks like whomever this was might have been murdered," Ashley said, pointing to a large knife wound through her ribs.

"Ok, so what are we supposed to do now?" Ashley said, looking at the skeleton before them. The friends looked at each other.

"The ghost said we need to figure out what happened and put things right to set her soul free. We need to look at all the clues and see if we can put together the story." Monica said, laying down everything she had found.

The three friends looked at all of the clues before them; the skeleton that had been stabbed, the letters to Marisa and Claire, the knife, the bloody shirt, the handkerchief and gloves and the candles.

It wasn't long before Monica had an idea. "I've got it. I think I know what happened and what we need to do." As soon as Monica finished speaking, the ghost of Marisa appeared before them.

Monica took a few minutes and explained to Marisa everything they had discovered and what they thought they needed to do. The ghost of Marisa smiled and laughed, then as quickly as she had arrived, she was gone.

Ashley went over to the entrance of the attic and was able to open it. The three friends proceeded to make good on their promise and set things right.

Well, they certainly found a lot of stuff. What did the friends put together from the clues they discovered, and what did they need to do to set things right? Once you think you know the answer, head to the ANSWER section of the book to see if you are correct.

CURIOUS CASE #8

The Murder on Morrison Rd

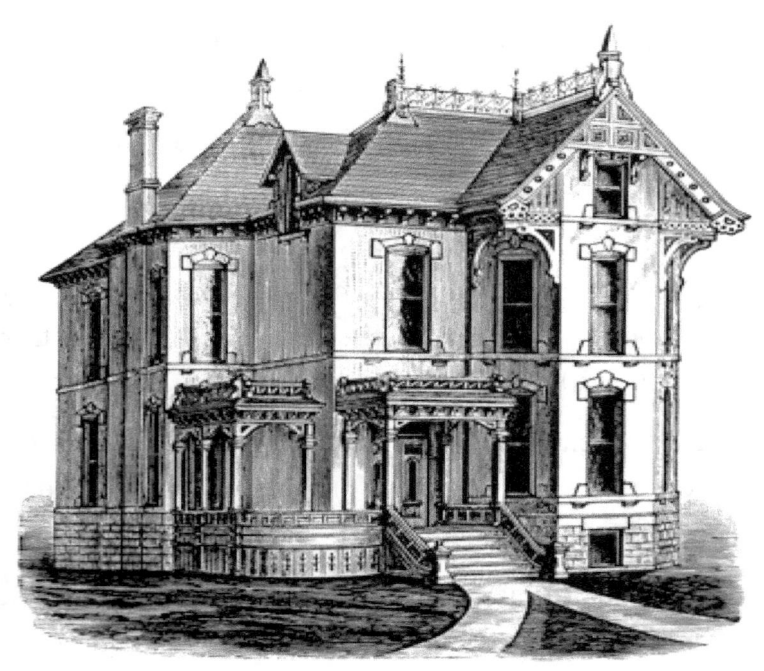

It was a beautiful day in October of 2015 when Lara and Stanley Sumner were getting ready for their dinner party. Lara and Stanley lived in a lovely home on a very exclusive street, Morrison Rd.

"Stanley, are you nearly ready? Our friends will be here soon." Lara called to her husband from the living room. "Yes, I'll be down in a moment," Stanley replied from upstairs.

Stanley had barely gotten downstairs when the doorbell rang, causing their little dog, Rufus, to bark wildly. Lara shot Stanley a look, then went over to answer the door. "Carla, Marcus! Please come in." Lara said, letting in the first of their guests to arrive. Stanley picked up Rufus and carried him to the kitchen to get him out of the way.

Carla and Marcus made their way to the living room, where Stanley was waiting for them. Lara entered the room, ready to join them; when the doorbell rang again, Rufus let out a howl and ran for the door. "Be right back!" She said as she made her way back to the door.

A few moments later, Lara returned to the living room with Anna, Isabelle, Eric and Greg. "Hey! Welcome! Grab a drink, grab a seat! We'll sit down to dinner once everyone arrives." Stanley said, greeting their friends.

Ding Dong. "I'll get it!" Stanley said to Lara as she was about to get up and get the door. Rufus howled, and Lara, having had enough, put Rufus outside while Stanley made his way to the front hall.

Stanley opened the door to reveal the remaining guests. "Hey, hey! Welcome friends. Come on in, grab a drink. We'll have dinner soon." Stanley let Erin, Shannon, Brett and Kevin in before closing the door and locking it.

The 12 friends were enjoying drinks in the living room when Lara clinked her glass. "All right, friends, it's time for dinner. Let's head into the dining room." All of the friends continued chatting as they made their way into the dining room.

"I've put out name tags, find your name and take your seats," Lara said, sitting at the head of the table. Everyone looked around for their names and then sat down in the appropriate spots.

The table was laid out as follows; Lara at the top of the table with Erin, Kevin, Isabelle, Marcus and Eric down her right-hand side and Shannon, Greg, Anna, Carla and Brett on her left-hand side. Stanley was seated at the other end of the table.

The friends began to eat and laugh and were having an all-around good time when suddenly, for no apparent reason, the lights went out.

"What happened?" A female voice said. "Did someone

turn the lights off?" A different female voice asked. "I think the power went out." A male voice replied. As all the friends murmured about the lights being out, there was a muffled man's scream. "What was that?" A woman said. "Oh my god, Stanley!" A man said.

Just as suddenly as the lights had gone off, they came back on and there, lying on the floor, was the body of Stanley Sumner, stabbed to death.

"Stanley! Stanley!" Lara screamed and ran over to Stanley. She hugged him tight, but he was gone, and she started sobbing uncontrollably. Carla came over and put a hand on Lara's shoulder; she turned to hug her crying uncontrollably.

"Who did this? How did this happen? Someone call the police!" Lara said through sobs. Everyone pulled out their phones only to discover they had no service. "I don't have service; that's weird." Said Brett. "Me either." Added Shannon. It became clear that no one had service. "The power outage must have knocked out cell service," Kevin commented.

Struck with the realization that they couldn't phone the police, they had to devise another plan. "Should one of us drive to the police station?" Marcus asked, getting ready to head for his car. "No. No one leaves. One of you murdered my husband." Lara said, almost screaming.

"Well, how are we supposed to figure out who did it? We aren't cops. We can't take fingerprints." Erin said shakily. Everyone nodded in agreement: everyone but Lara.

"None of us are leaving until we know what happened, so we better get to solving this," Lara said, looking suspiciously at her supposed friends.

No one liked the idea of being thought of as a murderer, but it looked like they didn't really have a choice. "Ok. Where do we begin? What are we supposed to do?" Kevin said, sitting back down in his seat.

"I think the best way to start is for everyone to say exactly what they were doing when the lights went out; maybe that will give us some insight into what was going on," Anna said very level-headedly.

"Agreed. That's as good as any place to start." Lara agreed. "I'll go first. I was pouring myself a glass of wine when the lights went out. You can see that I ended up spilling it all over the tablecloth." Lara showed everyone the stain on the tablecloth from the spill.

"I was eating when the lights went out. I nearly choked in shock." Anna said, giving her answer.

"We were having a conversation about work," Shannon said, motioning to herself and Greg. "Yes, we were talking about a new product that Shannon's store started carrying,"

Greg added.

"Carla, what about you?" Lara asked. "I was serving myself more potatoes when the lights went out. Look at my plate; I ended up with a huge mound of potatoes because I couldn't see what I was doing."

"I was feeding carrots to the dog under the table. He ran off with one. I hope that's ok." Brett said sheepishly. "I'm not a big fan of carrots, but I didn't want to offend."

"Erin? Kevin? What do you have to say for yourselves." Lara said, turning to her guests. "We were actually talking about vacations. I was recently in Italy." Erin said, "And I was recently in France." Kevin added. "So we were comparing travel notes." Erin finished.

"I was eating, the food was so good, and I was starving. Look at my plate; it's empty!" Isabelle said with a little sheepish giggle.

"Marcus and I were having an argument at the time. A friendly one but an argument nonetheless." Eric said to the group. "That's right, Eric and I were arguing about politics. It was nothing serious, but we were definitely in the midst of a conversation when the lights were out." Marcus added.

"Ok. Thank you. So everyone had an excuse, and no one could have done it." Anna said, exasperated. Lara stood up abruptly. "I know who did it. One of you is lying about what you were doing."

And with that, Lara began to explain who was lying and how she knew.

So, Detective, who was lying and who killed Stanley? Once you think you know the answer, head to the ANSWER section of the book to see if you're correct.

CURIOUS CASE #9

The Bank Heist

It was a cold rainy day in June 1895 when the Bay Street Boys set out to rob the National Trust Bank. The team consisted of six experienced bank robbers who were ready to pull off the biggest heist of their lives.

Each of the six men was well-trained and had a very specific role. William was the leader and the one responsible for making all the plans and ensuring the robbery went off without a hitch. Darwin was the driver; his job was to load everything in and out and be ready while the rest of the team completed the robbery. Benjamin and Carson were responsible for emptying the cash; it was up to them to ensure they got all of the cash as quickly as possible. Leonard was the lock breaker, it was up to him to break into the vault as quickly as possible, and he was a master of his trade. Lastly, there was Albert, and his job was crowd control; it was up to him to keep everyone calm and quiet in any way necessary.

The six men got into the getaway carriage, and Darwin loaded everything into the back. Once they arrived at the bank, the five members of the crew jumped out while Darwin waited for them to return with the money.

William was the first into the bank, "Everybody down on the floor, now!" He shouted, firing one shot into the air. Everyone fell to the ground almost instantly, and the crew went to work.

Albert walked through the bank holding his gun at the

ready to ensure that no one got up and everyone remained quiet.

William stood at the door, keeping a lookout to ensure that no one was on to them and that no one was coming into the bank.

Darwin sat in the carriage, keeping the horse ready for what he hoped would be a quick getaway.

Leonard went to the vault and got to work on getting it open, he was an expert safe cracker, but even he took a few minutes to get into the safe.

While Leonard worked on the safe, Benjamin and Carson were busy emptying the cash out of the teller's desks; they each had a bag full of money ready to go by the time Leonard had the safe cracked.

"I'm in! Let's go!" Leonard called to Benjamin and Carson, who dropped off the full bags of cash with William before heading to the safe with three new bags.

It wasn't long before Benjamin, Leonard, and Carson had emptied every dollar out of the safe and filled all three bags with cash.

"Someone's coming! We gotta split!" William called to the others from the doorway. Benjamin, Carson and Leonard ran from the safe, each carrying a bag of cash. Albert backed slowly through the crowd towards the front door and picked up one of the bags of cash on the ground; William grabbed the final bag.

The five bank robbers ran down the steps at the front of the bank, tossed the five bags of cash into the waiting carriage, and then entered and closed the door.

Darwin flicked the reins, and they were off down the street just before the police arrived. Darwin was an incredible getaway drive and took the carriage down side streets and back alleys, ensuring there was absolutely no way they could be followed.

Finally, after driving for about 30 minutes, Darwin made his way to their hideout that was on an old, beaten-down road just outside of town.

The group got out of the carriage, and everyone grabbed their equipment to take with them back inside. Once they were out, Darwin hid the carriage around back then the others met him to remove the bags of cash from inside.

Once inside, the robbers opened the bags and dumped two of the bags on the ground. One bag contained cash. The other was full of rocks and pieces of paper.

"What? What is this? Where's the money?" William said, throwing one of the rocks and breaking a window. They dumped the other three bags and found they were full of money, as expected, but why was one of the bags full of paper and rocks?

"Who's bag was that? Who stole the money? Our money. My money!" William shouted, throwing another rock through a window.

"Take it easy. Breaking windows isn't going to help anything." Leonard said, removing the pile of rocks so William couldn't throw anymore.

"Right. Well, whose bag was that?" William growled, wishing he had a rock to throw.

"How are we supposed to know? All the bags look identical, and besides, none of us were alone when we were collecting money." Carter said, perplexed.

"You're right, none of us were alone when we were collecting the money, but I think I know what happened," Benjamin said incredulously.

They are all criminals, but only one was responsible for the double cross. Who stole the money, and how did they do it? Once you think you know the answer, head to the ANSWER section of the book to see if you are correct.

CURIOUS CASE #10

The Dragon and The Unicorn

Long ago, on a far-off island, there lived creatures the likes of which no human has ever set eyes on. This magical island was run by two best friends, the dragon and the unicorn.

The unicorn was known for being kind, talkative and trustworthy, while the dragon was known for being brave forgetful and friendly. The two were the perfect complement to each other and were well-loved by all the mythical creatures that inhabited the island.

Living on a magical island meant the creatures had nothing to do but enjoy themselves. They ate well, they played, and every night they would have a party hosted by the dragon and the unicorn.

Because the mythical creatures had everything they could need in the world, gems and riches meant nothing to them, but some things still had sentimental value. The dragon and the unicorn each possessed a gem that meant more to them than life itself. The dragon had an emerald, and the unicorn had a ruby.

One evening after a long rainy day, the dragon and the unicorn were hosting their nightly party when the dragon realized that something was missing; his emerald was gone.

The dragon quickly stopped the celebration to ask his friends if they had seen it. Not a single one admitted to seeing it, which confused the dragon. Emeralds *don't simply disappear, or do they?* He thought to himself.

The dragon took a deep breath and then spoke, "My emerald is always kept in the same spot on the shelf in the great hall, next to the unicorn's ruby." Said the dragon calmly.

"But it is not always there. At night when you sleep, you always put it beside your bed." said the unicorn calmly. The dragon puffed some smoke. "That is correct, but I put it back out every morning when I awaken." He rebutted, feeling frustrated.

"Sometimes you leave it in the sitting room." said a centaur. "And sometimes you loan it to the children to play with." added the jackalope. "We have even seen you wear it around your neck." stated the Pegasus.

The dragon was silent for a moment. They were right. They were all right. He liked to think he had a routine, but he was so forgetful that the emerald could be anywhere. But then he thought about it some more. "That is how one of you stole it! You are using my forgetful ways to make me THINK that I lost it, but one of you, one of my supposed friends, has taken it, and I will indeed find out who." The dragon fumed and flew away, leaving all of the mythical creatures stunned.

Later that day, the dragon rounded up all of his closest 'friends' and began interrogating them about what they were doing when the emerald went missing. The first in the hot seat was the jackalope. "Tell me, Jackalope, what were you doing when the emerald went missing?" the dragon demanded.

The jackalope hopped forward and replied, "I was in my home, making the delicious carrot stew that I brought to the party." he stated before silently returning to his spot in the crowd.

The dragon huffed and continued. "How about you, Centaur." The centaur trotted forward. "I was enjoying a gallop through the hills." said the centaur calmly before trotting back to his spot in the group.

The dragon nodded, then calmly continued. "Pegasus, what do you have to say for yourself?" The Pegasus dramatically soared through the air before landing in front of the Dragon. "I was in the stables drying my wings and enjoying a feast of hay and oats." the Pegasus finished speaking and dramatically flew through the air before landing back in his spot.

The dragon turned to his best friend, the unicorn, "And you? What were you doing?" The unicorn was taken aback by the accusation by his so-called best friend, but he took a deep breath and calmly replied. "I, my friend, was with you. I saw you take the emerald from your bedside and place it in the great hall. Then I went to prepare for the party, leaving you alone with the emerald." the unicorn said calmly but sternly.

The dragon understood what he meant with his statement. He was accusing HIM of being responsible for the disappearance of the emerald; how dare he. The dragon took a deep breath and continued with his last suspect, the ogre.

"Ogre, where were you when my emerald was taken?" the dragon said gruffly. "When your emerald went missing, I was searching for more stones in the caves. In fact..." the ogre rummaged in his deep dirty pockets. "I have this if you would like it." The ogre pulled a brand new shiny emerald out of his pocket.

The dragon took the emerald from the ogre and examined it. It was a beautiful emerald, but it was not his. He handed it back. "Thank you, but I now know who is lying and is responsible for the theft of my emerald, and I intend to have it returned to me before the day is done."

All the mythical creatures looked at each other and then looked back at the dragon, eager to hear what he was going to say.

So there you have it. All of the mythical creatures claim not to be responsible, but one of them certainly is. Who was responsible for taking the emerald? Was it the jackalope, the centaur, the Pegasus, the unicorn, the ogre or even the dragon himself? Once you think you know the answer, head to the ANSWER section of the book to see if you are correct.

ANSWER SECTION

CURIOUS CASE #1

The Sword of Hawthorne

Where was the sword of Hawthorne hidden?

As Evie led the way down the hallway, the others followed. It was clear she knew where she was going even if they didn't.

Evie ran to the end of the hallway and was practically at the back door when Jamie called out to her, "Evie! Stop!

Where are you going?"

Evie stopped and turned to her friends. "Where did we see dark water? Remember? Before we entered the castle, we saw dark water in…." The realization suddenly hit Marcus.

"The fountain! The fountain out back was full of dark water." Marcus said in surprised excitement. "and it's on the west side of the castle, right outside the backdoor!"

"Yes, of course! The sword must be there." Lindsey added as she pushed hard on the back door. It took all of the friends together to force the old door open.

The friends ran out of the castle and saw the old fountain full of dark water just beyond the door. "There, the sword must be in there," Evie said, leaning over the fountain and looking inside.

"How are we supposed to get it out?" Jamie said, already knowing the answer. "One of us has to go in, don't we." She continued looking around at her friends.

Silence. No one was volunteering to get into a fountain full of dark water and who knows what else. Finally, Arlo cleared his throat. "I'll do it." He said, stepping forward.

Arlo took off his heavy outer clothes and sat on the side of the fountain with his feet dangling in the freezing cold water. "Ok, when you get in, you're going to have to move fast, that water is cold and dark, and who knows what is in there," Evie said, patting Arlo on the back.

He nodded in agreement and jumped in. Not realizing how deep the water would be, Arlo went right under, disappearing from view. "Arlo! Arlo!" Marcus shouted.

Moments later, Arlo reappeared, covered in slime and goo. "It's so deep and so cold. I don't think I will be able to find the sword." He called to his friends with his voice shivering.

"The middle! Go to the middle. I feel like there will be a ledge there." Lindsey said excitedly. Arlo began swimming to the middle of the fountain, and suddenly he stood up. There was, in fact, a ledge in the middle.

"You were right! There's a ledge right in the middle." Arlo said excitedly. He began to carefully move around the ledge when he felt something. "I think I found it!" Arlo shouted excitedly. "But I can't grab it. It's stuck!" Arlo said while struggling with the sword. "I'm going to need some help!"

The others looked at one another and knew what they had to do. They all removed their heavy outer layers and slowly got into the fountain. They swam to the middle of the fountain and joined Arlo on the ledge.

"Do you feel it?" Arlo asked as all of the friends felt around for the sword. "Yup!" "Got it!" They replied, each getting a grip on the sword.

"Ok, on three, we all pull together. One. Two. Three!" Arlo counted down as all of the friends pulled hard and managed to remove the sword from the holder.

"It's out. We did it!" Evie said with pure glee. The group each held part of the sword and awkwardly swam to the edge of the fountain. They heaved the heavy sword out of the water then all got out of the fountain, breathless and cold.

They quickly put their warm outer layers back on and then went over to the sword to check it out. Using a sleeve of his shirt, Marcus removed some of the sludge from the sword revealing the precious stones that encased it.

"We found it! I can't believe we found it!" Lindsey said, hugging Jamie with excitement.

"I know! I can't believe it!" Jamie said, returning the hug.

"We did it! But now we have a bigger problem." Evie said, looking at her friends. "What?!" Marcus said, exasperated.

"How do we get this thing outta here? Do you think an Uber can pick us up?" Evie said half-jokingly.

The friends looked at each other. Evie was right. They had the sword, but now they had to get it home. So the friends packed up their stuff, each grabbed a part of the sword and began the long walk back to the Beamich.

The End

CURIOUS CASE #2

The Witch's Curse

What did Jacob do to break the curse?

Jacob ran from his home as fast as he could. If he was right, he would be able to save his entire family before it was too late.

As Jacob ran down the path, he bumped into many of his neighbours, who were quite annoyed with his discourteous attitude.

After only a few minutes, Jacob arrived at his store, the thing he loved most. "Excuse me, pardon me." Jacob pushed through the patrons that had been waiting around in hopes that he would be opening soon.

He unlocked the door and went inside; he made his way straight to the alcohol he kept at the back of his shop. He immediately opened the bottles and began pouring them all over the store, covering every shelf and every corner.

Jacob grabbed a box of matches and then made his way to the front of the store, pouring alcohol right to the doorway. Jacob stepped outside and turned to the crowd that had gathered. "Please, ladies and gentlemen, back up as far as you can." Jacob sounded quite frantic as he yelled to the crowd.

The onlookers slowly backed up and most left the area entirely. Once Jacob was sure no one was close enough to get hurt, he struck a match and dropped it in the doorway. Jacob backed up as he watched his store, the thing he loved most, burn to the ground.

As he was standing and watching his store burn, he heard the witch's voice in his head. "You have destroyed the thing you love most. The curse is lifted."

Jacob broke out of the trance he had been in while watching his store burn and realized he had to get home to his family.

Jacob ran down the path back to his home and burst through the door. "Julianna! Frederick! Maria!" Jacob called out to his family. At first, there was no reply, and Jacob's heart sank; had he failed? Had he lost everything? Then, just as Jacob was about to give up, he heard Julianna's sweet little voice, "Father, what is wrong?" Jacob looked up to see his family waking from the curse as if nothing had happened.

"You're alive; you're all alive!" Jacob ran other and hugged his family, who were all confused and groggy but otherwise unharmed. "Jacob, what is happening? Why are you not at the store?" Maria said, thoroughly confused.

"The store is gone, and everything will be fine from now on, I promise you. I promise all of you." Jacob gave his family another tight squeeze and cried tears of joy. The curse had indeed been broken.

The End

CURIOUS CASE #3

The Pirate's Revenge

How could Bart the Beast carry out his curse even after his death?

As soon as the pirates fled the island, a figure appeared in the distance. Life had been hard on him; he was aged beyond his years from what had clearly been a long hard life.

"Is it done? Are they gone?" An even older man asked.

"Yes, Artemis, they are gone. The island is still ours." Claudio replied with a tired sigh.

Artemis and Claudio shook hands; even after more than 50 years, they had managed to keep the promise their father made all those years ago. You see, Anabella and her boys escaped the night before Bart the Beast was overthrown, but they did not go far.

Bart's loving family remained just out of sight and witnessed all the torture Bart was subjected to; they also heard his promise.

As soon as it was safe to do so, Anabella and her boys got to work avenging Bart's death, and years later, after Anabella's death, Claudio and Artemis continued to stand guard over the island to ensure that no pirate ever lay claim to it again. In fact, no one has dared to set foot on the island for more than 150 years for fear that the curse might still exist.

The End

CURIOUS CASE #4

The Lost Pyramid

How did Eliza find the treasure of Ra?

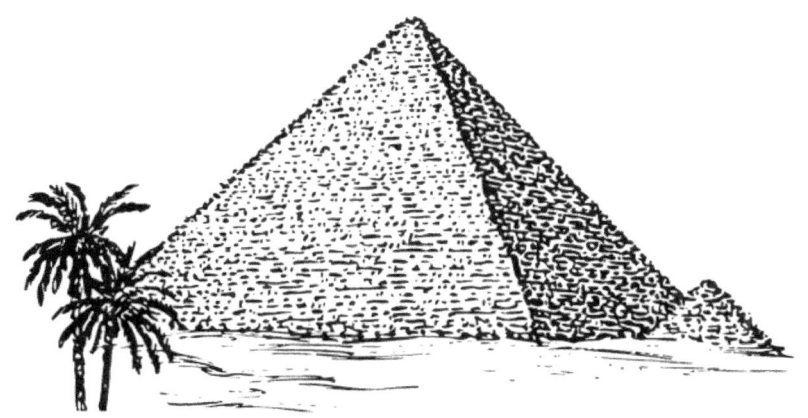

It was fifteen years after the discovery of the treasure when Eliza was giving a speech to fellow archeologists about the significance of her find. Once she completed her rehearsed speech, she opened the floor for questions.

A young woman raised her hand, "Yes, you in the back; what's your question?" Eliza asked. The young woman stood up and asked. "How did you come to find the treasure? You have spoken extensively about the treasure itself but not how you were able to find it when so many others had failed." The young woman sat down, giving the floor to Eliza to answer.

"What an excellent question; allow me to explain. My Uncle Gerald was actually at the heart of this discovery. He had found every piece of information I needed to find the treasure, but one detail was incorrect. You see, the stars were an important element in the discovery of the treasure, the most important element. In fact, but Gerald did not factor in the movement of the Earth between ancient times and now. The North Star was not where it is now thousands of years ago. Once I considered this, I was able to hypothesize where the North Star would have been in the time the treasure was hidden, and once I figured that out, I could locate it."

Everyone in the audience was in awe. Who would have thought the slight movement of the Earth over thousands of years would have impacted finding the treasure that much?

The End

CURIOUS CASE #5

The Invasion

Plutonium does, in fact, exist, so why didn't these two brilliant scientists have any idea what the Neptunians were talking about?

This mystery is a bit different than the other as the answer lies in knowledge outside of the story. If you remember correctly, this tale was set in 1939, and even though Plutonium did, of course, exist at this time, it was discovered one year later, in 1940. Maybe our two scientist friends ended up being involved in its discovery!

The End

CURIOUS CASE #6

The Forbidden Temple

Which hallway did they choose? The dead end, the bottomless pit, the pit of spikes or the pit of poisonous snakes?

The explorers met again in the main hall to discuss what they had found and decide on their best option. Each of them told the others what they had seen so they could weigh their choices.

"I know which way to go, it is unpleasant, but we will be able to leave unharmed," Peter said excitedly. "The hallway I went down ended in a pit of poisonous snakes, but since the temple has been locked up for 3000 years, all of the snakes are dead."

The others looked at Peter with a mix of joy and relief; thankfully, they would be able to escape the temple! The group followed Peter down the corridor and to the edge of the snake pit. They looked inside and observed that the snakes were all, in fact, dead. They climbed in one by one and waded through the pit full of skeletons and preserved snake flesh.

Once they reached the far side, they pulled themselves out before continuing down the hallway. They walked for only a few moments before they reached what appeared to be another door. They worked together to push and shove until, like with the front entrance, they managed to open the door just enough to escape.

The End

CURIOUS CASE #7

The Ghost in the Attic

What did the friends put together from the clues they discovered, and what did they need to do to set things right?

The friends very carefully brought the clues out of the attic, then went up and picked up the skeleton and carefully brought that down as well. They laid the skeleton on the floor next to the pile of clues.

"Ok, that was disturbing. What are we supposed to do now?" Ashley said to the others. "Well, we know that Marisa killed Claire using a knife. And from the letters, we know it's because Marisa thought her husband, Jack Jovin, JJ, was cheating on her with Claire. Roland Matthew Derby, also known as R.D., was responsible for all this." Monica said as Ashley and Jillian nodded in agreement.

"Yes, and we know that Claire loved roses, so we should bury her in the rose garden," Jillian added. "There is a beautiful rose garden in our backyard that's been here since we bought the house."

The three friends gingerly carried the skeleton down the stairs and into the backyard. They then dug a hole next to the roses and buried the skeleton.

As soon as they filled in the hole, the sky lit up, and the ghosts of Marisa and Claire hugged, peace at last.

The End

Curious Case #8

The Murder on Morrison Rd

Who was lying and killed Stanley?

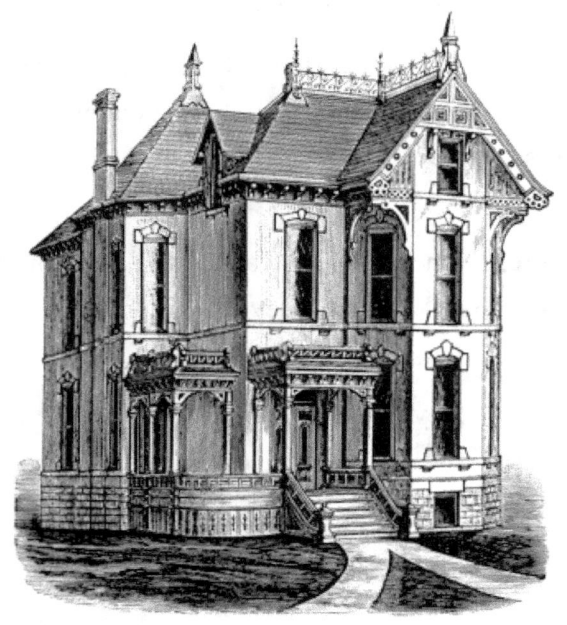

Lara stood next to Stanley's body and looked at her friends. "I know which of you is lying, but I'm going to give you a chance to come clean before I reveal your guilt to the others." Silence. "Very well, then you leave me no choice. Brett, you are guilty of killing Stanley; your alibi could not possibly be true." Lara said, moving towards Brett.

Brett, not appreciating the accusations, backed up. "What? That's ridiculous! I didn't kill Stanley! How dare you accuse me of that!" Brett was getting defensive, but Lara wasn't backing down.

"What was it you said you were doing when Stanley was murdered? Feeding the dog under the table. Well, you might not have realized this, but I put Rufus outside just as all of you were arriving. There is no way you were feeding him under the table." Lara had now backed Brett into the corner.

Brett was shocked and speechless; the guilt was written all over his face. "How could you? How dare you?" Lara was getting emotional in the face of her husband's killer. Just as she was about to completely lose it on him, Erin interrupted. "Phones are back; I'm calling the police!"

Marcus and Kevin forced Brett into a chair and tied him up; now, all they had to do was wait for the police to arrive and arrest Brett since Stanley's murderer had already been found.

The End

Curious Case #9

The Bank Robbery

Who stole the money, and how did they do it?

All of the robbers sat down as Benjamin gave his theory about what he thought happened. "So, as I already said, none of us were alone with the money when it was in the bank, but one of us was alone with the money after we left." The robbers all looked at each other, unsure of what he was talking about.

"When we arrived back at the hideout, Darwin let us out with all of our gear, then drove around to the back so we could unload the money. It was during that time that he switched one of the bags of money with a dummy bag. I bet if we look in the woods just behind the hideout, we will find it." Benjamin finished standing up.

The robbers went out back, and it didn't take them 5 minutes to locate the bag of money, hidden just out of sight. "Well, Darwin. What do you have to say for yourself?" Benjamin asked as the robbers encircled Darwin.

"Fine, it was me. I've been skimming money out of the bags for years, and since none of you were smart enough to realize that, I figured none of you were smart enough to catch me." Darwin said, trying to back away with no luck. It was clear Darwin's time as a bank robber was up, and he wasn't sure if his life might be up too.

The End

Curious Case #10

The Dragon and the Unicorn

What happened to the emerald?

The dragon let out a puff of smoke followed by a blast of fire. "Thank you all for being honest and telling me where you were when my emerald went missing. I know one of you was lying and therefore is responsible for taking my precious emerald." The dragon stepped forward towards the group and then dramatically turned to face the centaur.

"You told us you were galloping in the hills when my emerald was stolen, but that could not be possible. At the time my emerald was stolen, there was a terrible storm. There is no way you could have been out galloping in the open at that time." The dragon was now nose-to-nose with his supposed friend.

The centaur was silent for a moment, then reached into his fur and pulled out the emerald. "I am sorry. I do not know why I stole it or why I lied about stealing it. Can you forgive me, my friend?" The centaur said, bowing down to the dragon.

The dragon stood silent for a moment, then accepted the emerald from the centaur. "Your apology is accepted, my friend." The dragon and the centaur shared a moment, and it was clear that their friendship had been restored.

The dragon replaced the emerald with its rightful place and then began preparing for their nightly party.

The End

For now...